The Fall of Corey

By

Eric Burton

Chapter 1

The Trojan senior captains called for captain's practice in July of 2019, and Corey and Travis, now sophomores, were looking for respect from the upperclassmen. Corey and Travis hustled with everything they had, and seniors were quick to view the boys as equals. Corey and Travis distinguished themselves from the other quarterbacks and running backs with the guidance of Coach McNally, Travis's father. Coach McNally was a coach of the Trojans from 2016 to 2018, but he left the team December of 2018 after an argument with Head Coach Galanos. Even though he was not there to directly guide them, Coach McNally helped the boys train hard all year round, and during the winter prior to the 2019 season, Corey and Travis separated themselves from the rest of the team. Though the senior captains didn't say anything of it during the winter, the seniors knew they were a separate caliber, and so did the rest of the team.

Double sessions began in August, and Corey and Travis demonstrated profound knowledge of the Trojan playbook, executing passing and running plays with explosiveness. Head

Coach Galanos was impressed with the boys, but Corey did not feel the coach was noticing them. Head Coach Galanos was a first generation Greek-American in his fifties, and he did not show his emotions to others, especially to children. Corey, on the other hand, was a boy of many moods and faces. When Corey felt discouraged, Travis was consistent in cheering him up, and on the field they propelled each other by tapping into each another's vaulting ambition. It was their vaulting ambitions that made them best friends.

The last Friday of summer was the last day of double sessions. Corey and Travis woke up at five like they had every other morning before doubles, warming themselves up with a run at the reservoir. Since they ran everyday, they were not sore after Friday's final session like some of the seniors and other varsity players. The boys waved as their teammates left the locker room, and when the boys finally had the chance to talk to Coach Galanos, the coach refused to tell them if they made the cut or not. The boys began to walk to Travis's house, and they entertained themselves with fantasies about what it would be like starting on varsity. As the sun began to set behind the trees,

Coach McNally found the boys. He pulled beside them in his truck. Coach McNally, Travis's father, yelled over to them.

"Get in boys, you're not going to believe this."

Corey and Travis jumped into the truck, Travis at his usual seat in the front, Corey behind him in the back.

"You're not going to believe it boys," Coach McNally said, "but I got the job with the Spartans."

"No way dad," Travis shouted in surprise, "that's awesome."

Corey listened as Coach McNally spoke quickly about coaching for the Spartans, and when coach transitioned the conversation to Travis switching schools, Corey grew anxious. Travis knew Corey was anxious by the tone of his voice, and Travis looked back at Corey, then back at his father.

"Maybe Corey can go with us," Travis offered, turning his head and smiling towards Corey. Corey returned Travis's smile.

"Maybe," Coach McNally said. "Corey, talk to your father tonight."

Travis got a text from one of the seniors captains, inviting the boys to a senior party to celebrate the end of double sessions.

Corey insisted they go out and celebrate Coach McNally's new job, and the coach recommended they go to Leo's Pizza. Coach McNally was willing to drop the boys off to the party, but Corey insisted they go out and discuss their football careers, and Travis agreed.

Corey and Travis took a seat by a window table while Coach McNally ordered the pizza. Travis texted the senior captain who had invited the boys to the party to let him know they would not be making it. Corey surfaced from his pocket a twenty-dollar bill when Coach McNally arrived to the table, and the coach insisted Corey put the dollar bill away. When Corey put his dollar bill away, Travis put his phone away. When Corey asked coach questions about what happened with him and the Trojans, Coach McNally answered, and Travis listened.

Coach McNally explained to the boys that he was chosen as the Trojan head coach during August 2016 when Corey's grandfather retired as head coach and gym teacher. According to Coach McNally, Corey's grandfather wanted him to become the next head coach and gym teacher. When Corey's grandfather insisted the school bring along Coach McNally as the coach, it was Corey's grandfather's hope that the school would father Coach McNally into the gym teacher position. Corey acknowledged he knew something of this, admitting that his grandfather never shared many of the details with him. Corey claimed that his grandfather did not want him to get involved in the politics, and for the most part, Corey listened and focused on his duties as a quarterback.

When Corey's grandfather passed in 2018, the story reminded untold. Now before Corey, there was a lead into a deeper story Corey never knew, and as he listened to Coach McNally explain the story, the ambitious quarterback felt an awakened passion for the truth.

Coach McNally continued that even though the Trojan gym position was open, the principal was not fond of McNally because of his name and the reputation of his cousins. Coach McNally was then refused an interview, and instead, Coach Galanos, the principal's brother in law, was offered the position. When Coach Galanos took over as head coach, Coach McNally dropped down to offensive coach, and the two coaches struggled to get along with each other. Coach Galanos became the head coach in August of 2018, and when Corey's grandfather passed in November, Coach McNally knew his time with the Trojans was limited. Coach McNally told the boys he quit December of the 2018 season because of politics. Corey asked for details, and Travis's ears were open, but Coach McNally refused to explain himself. When Travis asked his father about the Spartans, the conversation shifted and Corey listened as Travis and Coach McNally discussed transferring schools. When Corey became anxious from their conversation, Corey pulled his phone from his pocket and checked his social network for distractions.

"This is a new start Corey," said Coach McNally, finally to Corey. "I've been looking for something full time for three years, and honestly, it's going to put me and Travis in a better position."

"I understand coach," Corey said, lifting his eyes from his phone.

Travis watched Corey. Travis rose from his seat by his father and sat next to Corey, placing his arm around Corey's shoulder.

"We will work it out Corey," Travis said, smiling again at his best friend. "Just make sure you talk to your dad tonight."

Pizza was delivered to the table, and Travis continued to sit by Corey's side. Coach McNally suggested the boys watch the BU vs. Syracuse game tomorrow morning. As they spoke of college football, Corey began to feel better. Corey also felt better when Corey reminded him of their dream to play for Boston University. Though Corey began to feel better, he also thought of his father, and Corey wondered how he would tell his father about the Spartans. Travis noticed Corey's anxiety, but Travis did not ask Corey about it. Corey wanted to share what he was feeling with Travis and Coach McNally, but Corey knew this was something he would have to figure out on his own.

The sky was a dark blue, and the street was barely visible when they finished eating. Travis suggested that he and Corey still go to the senior party, but Corey insisted Coach McNally drive him home. Coach McNally drove the quarterback home, and Travis reminded Corey to call him in the morning. Travis suggested they train and run the reservoir in the morning. Corey agreed, stepping out of the truck. Corey waved to Coach McNally and Travis as they drove down the hill. He watched as Coach McNally's truck took a left on Grove Street.

Corey's parents were not home when he opened the door. When he went to his room, he rested on his bed and went into thinking about his football career. *Could I really make it in football without Travis? Could we really go to college together? Could I really leave the Trojans and everything my grandfather built to become a Spartan?* Corey thought about football and school and family, and he decided he would have to transfer and play with Travis and be a Spartan too. The Trojan quarterback decided he would have to become a Spartan and train with Travis under Coach McNally's wing. After all, it was Coach McNally who convinced the boys that they possessed the talent to play college football. Corey reminded himself that the dream to play at Boston University was a dream himself, Travis, and Coach McNally shared. Corey decided his father would have to accept it.

Corey's mother returned home at seven, and when Corey asked about his father, she told him he was out at the bar. Corey insisted he help her with dinner, and Corey began to boil two pots of water.

"Coach McNally got the job with Spartans mom" said Corey. "Travis will be going too. I want to go too mom."

"You know your father won't like that."

"But Coach McNally has been my coach since Pop Warner, and I want to play with Travis. We learned the game together."

"You know your grandfather wouldn't like that."

Corey wanted to tell his mother he did not care about his father's opinion. The Trojan quarterback wanted to tell his mother that his grandfather's opinion was irrelevant. Corey wanted to tell his mother what he wanted of his own career. He wanted to tell her all of this, but Corey did not want to argue with her. The son and quarterback opened the box of macaroni and cheese, and when the water turned to a boil, he tossed the macaroni into the pot. In the other pot, Corey began to steam hot dogs.

"Coach McNally told me I have what it takes to play in college mom," Corey continued. He took a seat at the kitchen table. "He would know mom, he played for Boston University. You know I'm gonna need scholarships to pay for college."

Corey's mother nodded and said nothing. She knew it was true. When Corey's mother continued to say nothing, Corey asked if he could help her with anything else. She declined. Corey watched as his mother stirred the macaroni and checked the hot dogs with a fork. When the garage opened, Corey and his mother jumped. The loving son insisted he help her set up the table, but his mother rushed him off, and Corey started for his room.

"I will let you know when dinner is ready Corey."

Corey rushed into his room and locked his door. Corey listened to his father's footsteps as he came in from the garage. He listened as the door rushed open. He listened as the door slammed shut. The Trojan quarterback listened as his mother asked why he had been out so late. He listened as his father's voice grew louder, and Corey listened as his mother's voice became softer. Corey felt a swell of fear when his mother brought up the Spartans. When his father rushed over, banging on his door, Corey rushed to his bed. Corey's father cursed at the locked door, and Corey jumped up from his bed and unlocked the door. Corey's father rushed in, and the Trojan quarterback took two steps back. Corey threw his open hands up.

"What is your mother telling me about you wanting to play for the Spartans?"

"Coach McNally-"

"I don't give a damn about Coach McNally," screamed Corey's father. "Your grandfather made the Trojans what they are. You're grandfather, 1965 Super Bowl champions, and the birth of Trojan football. As long as you're living in this household boy, as long as I'm paying your bills, you're playing for the Trojans. Now is that clear boy?" Corey's father stepped closer to Corey. The Trojan quarterback did not step back.

Corey waited, but his father did not hit him. Corey knew his father would not hit him, not after last time, not after the last time Corey's mother brought him to court. He wanted to comment about his father's breath, but Corey knew it would only fuel his father's anger. He wanted to tell his father Coach McNally was more of a father to him, but Corey knew it would not help. Corey waited. He said nothing. Corey's father then walked out of the room, and Corey closed the door, locking the lock, including the dead bolt. Corey rested on his bed and thought about how he would convince his parents to accept him and let him transfer to the Spartans. When his mother called, and dinner was ready, Corey unlocked his door and walked to the dinner table.

Corey attempted to help his mother set the dinner plates. Corey stopped when his father yelled at him. Corey's mother hurried and set the dinner table, and Corey's father served himself first.

"Do you know why Coach McNally left the Trojans boy," Corey's father grunted, staring at Corey. Corey shook his head, looking away. "Look at me when I speak to you boy," Corey's father shouted.

The quarterback shifted his head and looked at his mother, her eyes drawn to her meal. Emily saw Corey looking at her, and she took a small bite of her macaroni and cheese.

"Emily, tell Corey what Helen has been telling us." Corey's mother waited. Emily shook her head. Corey's father stomped his fists on the table. He let out a shout. "Fine, I will tell him."

"I don't care about the rumors," Corey said.

"They are not rumors boy. Now goddammit, listen."

Corey's father went to explain Helen's rumor. According to Helen, Coach McNally was touching her son Patrick prior to leaving the Trojans. According to Helen, this was the real reason Coach McNally left the team in 2018. According to Corey's father, Coach McNally wanted to leave the team before he got caught.

"I don't believe any of this," Corey mumbled.

"You better believe it boy," Corey's father said.

"The Spartans hired him to be their gym teacher and head coach," Corey added. "He got the job he wanted. People are just trying to sabotage him."

"Well, he won't be there long when the truth gets out."

"I don't believe any of this," Corey said. Corey wanted to let out a scream, but he knew it was what his father wanted him to do. Instead, Corey tightened his fists and shook his legs under the dinner table.

"Believe it boy," Corey's father said. "Helen is an honest woman." Corey's father stuffed a hot dog into his face. "I hope Coach McNally is not pulling any funny stuff on you boy," Corey's father said, still chewing.

Corey looked at his mother. He wished she would say something. Corey wanted his mother to say she knew Coach McNally, and that she knew he would never do such a thing. Corey wanted his mother to explain to Corey's father that when he wasn't around, Coach McNally, Jeff, was like a father for Corey. Corey hated how his mother always became so quiet when his father came home late from the bar, and Corey wished today she would speak up. Corey wanted to yell over to her, demanding that she speak up. Instead, Corey listened as his father continued about Helen's rumor. Corey gradually stopped listening to his words, and when he finished his plate, Corey rose from his seat.

"Salvatore," Corey shouted. "I don't care what you say about Coach McNally, and I don't care what you say about me going to the Spartans. I am going to the Spartans and I don't care if you like it or not!"

"Not as long as you're living in this house boy," said Corey's father. Corey's father rose from his seat. "As long as you're living in this house, you are a Trojan." Corey's father watched as his son walked towards his room. Corey watched as Salvatore's fingers gripped a porcelain plate.

"Salvatore!" Let's go out for a cigarette," Corey's mother screamed. Emily rose from her seat, blocking Corey from his father.

Corey's father released the porcelain plate. Salvatore walked to the porch with Emily. He kept his eyes on Corey. The Trojan quarterback walked quickly to his bedroom, locking his door, locking his dead bolt.

Corey knew his parents were back inside when he could smell their cigarettes. Corey knew his parents were done eating when he heard the water running. He knew his parents were not talking when he could only hear water running. When the Trojan quarterback heard footsteps at his door, he clutched onto his door nob, placing his weight against the door.

"Corey baby, it's just me," Corey's mother whispered. "I will talk to your father about the Spartans."

"Okay mom, thank you. Are you safe?"

"Yes Corey, I will be fine. Goodnight, I love you.

"I love you too mom." Corey wanted to hug and kiss his mother, but his anxiety would not allow him to unlock the door.

Corey waited until his mother left. Corey waited for the sound of more footsteps. When he heard no footsteps, Corey walked away from his door and rested in his bed. Corey thought about Travis's smile, and Corey was conscious when he felt his body relax. The quarterback thought about football, Coach McNally, Travis, and Boston University until he was too tired to think. He raised his blanket up to his face and breathed steadily. When tiredness overcame his anxiety, Corey fell asleep.

Chapter 2

Emily signed the papers necessary for Corey's transfer, and with the help of Coach McNally, Corey became a Spartan the second week of school. There was an argument between Corey's parents those transitioning weeks, but Corey was not home to witness it. His mother was selective when she shared the details of the argument, and Corey assumed the argument was related to him leaving the Trojans. Emily worked overtime to avoid Salvatore, and when Corey returned home most nights, he was alone. Corey hated being alone, and when he became too anxious, he slept over Travis's house. Corey was comforted by Travis's attention. On the Thursday before the Spartan's second game of the season, Corey returned home. He was happy when his mother was home. The Spartan quarterback helped his mother cook fish sticks and French fries, and as they cooked together, Emily explained to Corey that Salvatore was going to be away for a while. Corey had an idea of what she meant, and Corey wanted to confirm with her the reason of his absence. Corey was curious if his departure was connected to what happened five years ago, but he was too afraid to ask. He let himself believe his father was away for the same reason he had been away five years ago, and Corey kept his anxieties to himself. He wanted to admit his feelings to his mother, but he let himself become numb to the facts. Corey hoped Salvatore's absence would allow his mother to pursue her own happiness.

On the football field, the Spartan quarterback pushed himself, and so did Travis. When he felt discouraged, Travis reminded him of his talent. By their third week together as Spartans, Corey and Travis earned themselves second-string varsity positions. By their fourth game, their ability to work together and run effective plays became essential to the success of the varsity team. Corey became a leader in the huddle, calling plays and instilling faith in his teammates. Travis was as agile as a panther, breaking free from linemen and exploding through any hole, juking and stiff-arming himself out of any tackle. Corey and Travis proved to be vital to the varsity team, and at the end of their fifth game, the senior captains invited the boys to be part of the after game speech. For a moment, Corey and Travis were like upperclassmen, and the boys loved the fame.

Coach McNally concluded the speech that Friday night with his own acknowledgements, in addition to his own criticisms. After, the team dispersed and showered. Corey returned to his locker and found Travis showered and dressed, sitting on the bench near Corey's locker.

"Any plans for the weekend," Travis asked.

"No, not really," Corey replied.

"Any word on your dad?"

"No, not really."

"My dad and I are going to the BU game in the morning if you want to come along," said Travis. Travis rose from the bench. "Let's ask my dad, maybe you can stay over tonight."

"You ask him," Corey said. "You ask him and I will call my mom."

"Okay," Travis said, "I will meet you outside."

Corey finished changing and watched Travis walk away. The Spartan quarterback walked out of the locker room to call his mother. He noticed when Travis passed by him, and Corey watched his friend climb into the front seat of Coach McNally's truck.

"That's fine Corey," Corey's mother said over the phone. "You go and have fun."

"What about you mom, what are you going to do?"

"Dr. Hamilton asked if I could help cover the third shift. There was a call out, and we could really use the money."

"Okay," Corey said. "I will talk to you tomorrow. I love you mom."

"I love you too Corey, be safe."

Corey hung up his phone and shoved his phone back into his front pocket. Corey opened the truck and took his seat behind Travis.

"My dad will be right out," Travis said. "He's just locking up." Corey watched Travis go onto his phone.

Corey thought about telling Travis then about Salvatore, and what he had done to him five years ago, but Corey did not want Travis to think differently of him. Five years ago when Corey's father went away, it took everything of Corey to keep it to himself. The last thing Corey wanted was to be a victim, and in his anxiety, Corey fell silent behind Travis. The Spartan quarterback passed the time in silence, pulling his phone from his pocket, browsing his social network for distractions. When Travis put his phone down, he looked behind at Corey. Travis smiled, and Corey smiled and laughed. Travis asked Corey if he remembered those nights eight years ago when him and Coach McNally used to spend weekends at the Cape, and Corey nodded, smiling in remembrance. Corey followed Travis as he recalled those summer nights, listening to Coach McNally talk about Boston University. Corey and Travis recalled those summer nights when they fantasied football scholarships and college fame. As they continued about Boston University, Travis explained to Corey that his father was planning a trip for the team to see a BU game. Corey became so excited of the news that he let out a high pitch laugh, and when Travis laughed, Corey laughed at himself.

Corey watched as Coach McNally left the locker room alongside a Spartan assistant coach. He looked at Travis and pointed to Coach McNally. The Spartan quarterback pointed out that Coach McNally's face had a queer expression to it.

Coach McNally opened the truck door and sat in the driver's seat. "You're not going to believe it boys," Coach

McNally said. The coach fastened his seatbelt. "Boston University scouts are coming out to watch the St. John's game in two weeks."

Corey and Travis looked at each other. Their faces began to beam.

"This is it baby," Travis yelled. Corey laughed at Travis, and Travis hit Corey on the shoulder.

Corey smiled when Travis smiled at him. Travis asked his father about the scouts, and Coach McNally admitted he did not know, admitting he only knew that they would be there. Corey asked questions about Boston University, and Coach McNally reminded him again of his championship career in 87-88, reminding Corey again that he tore his ACL during the Super Bowl of his senior year. Corey continued to ask about Boston University, and Coach McNally answered. Travis offered what he could remember about his father's Boston University days, and when Travis was wrong with his facts, Coach McNally corrected him with a fatherly compassion. Corey did not admit it, but Corey was jealous of Travis and the attention Coach McNally was giving him. When Coach McNally confirmed the boys were both elite athletics, Corey felt confident, and Travis enhanced his encouragement. Travis reminded Corey that he was the kind of running back he was because of Corey's leadership as a quarterback.

Coach McNally drove off into the night, and Corey and Travis fantasied about their football dreams and futures. Corey reminded himself of how grateful he was of Travis, Coach McNally, and their undying dream. Corey banished his jealousy.

The Spartan quarterback fell silent after fifteen minutes into the car ride. Corey rolled down his window, welcoming the October breeze onto his face. Coach McNally turned up the radio, and Coach McNally and Travis went on about a new rock band that was playing a show in Boston soon. Coach McNally asked if Corey was interested in the band, and Corey agreed. Corey then discontinued the conversation, and Corey listened as Coach McNally and Travis went on about it. Corey listened for a few minutes before his thoughts possessed him.

Corey reminded himself of how happy he was to be with Coach McNally and Travis. Corey felt grateful his father was out of the picture again, and Corey hoped his mother would pursue her own happiness. Corey hoped that his mother would make it to the St. John's game. When Corey thought of his mother working long hours at the Trojan Residential House, the quarterback's hopes began to dim. Corey knew his mother had to work those hours. Corey knew his mother had to work those hours to pay the bills. Corey knew all this, but the Spartan quarterback held on to his hope that his mother would make the game in two weeks. Corey reminded himself of his dream with Travis and Coach McNally, and Corey saw tonight's game as a manifestation of that dream, and Corey felt renewed.

Coach McNally pulled the truck into the driveway. Before the garage door could close, Travis dragged Corey into the living room. Travis showed Corey a new video console Coach McNally was able to buy with the Spartan money, and while Corey was jealous, the quarterback was also happy for his friend. Travis turned on the console and showed Corey how to create his own character on a new college football video game. Travis made himself into a character with maxed stats, and Corey made a quarterback that resembled Travis. The boys played side by side for two games, and when they went into a verses exhibition, Travis dominated Corey in the virtual football world. Coach

McNally went off to shower and Corey watched as the coach

walked past him. Corey studied Coach McNally's step. Corey

watched when Coach McNally returned, blankets and pillows in

his hands. Corey took the blankets and pillows from Coach

McNally's hands.

"You can sleep on the couch Corey," Coach McNally said.

Coach McNally scanned the couch to make sure Corey had what

he needed. "Boys, don't stay up too late, we're leaving first thing

in the morning for Boston."

Corey and Travis nodded. Corey watched as Coach

McNally walked upstairs to his bedroom. Corey thought of the

rumor, and for a moment, Corey shivered. Corey shivered and the

Spartan quarterback looked to see if Travis noticed him. Travis

did not. Corey wanted to ask Travis if he had heard of the rumor,

but Corey did not want to upset his best friend. Corey did not

want to upset his best friend with something that probably was

not true. Corey thought about that Friday night in late August

when Corey's father gave him the sick news, and Corey began to

remember other nights his father returned home from the bar

intoxicated. As Corey remembered those nights, his thoughts

became miserable, and Travis watched Corey's decline in his game play. Corey made a comment of how poor he was at using the controls, and Travis made no comment. Corey wished Travis would make a comment, but Corey was confident Travis would not break their bro code. Travis rose from the coach and Corey made an inaudible sigh.

"See you in the morning Corey," said Travis. Travis shut off the television, and Corey watched as he tucked the game console away. Travis gathered his belongings. "See you in the morning Corey," Travis said again. "You have everything you need?"

Corey reviewed his pillows and blankets and nodded. Corey watched as Travis walked away. Corey hoped Coach McNally had been good to him.

When Corey knew he was alone, he shut the lights off in the living room and rested himself on the couch. When Corey's mind would not stop racing, he searched online for his grandfather. *Troy Aeneas, 1965 Super Bowl.* Corey again began to question himself.

What if my father was right? What if papa Aeneas wanted me to play for the Trojans?

Corey grew anxious as his thoughts slipped away. When Corey remembered Travis, Coach McNally, and football scholarships, Corey reminded himself he made the right decision. Corey reminded to himself that him and Travis were signed onto a dream, and their dream was soon to come true.

Corey closed his eyes and allowed himself to set into Coach McNally's pillows. He rolled on to his side, and after thinking about football and Travis, Corey fell asleep.

Chapter Three

The air was cool when they arrived into Boston Saturday morning. Coach McNally led the boys to his favorite bakery before they went into the stadium, explaining that the pastries near the school were the biggest and best in the city.

"After the game I will show you around the school, so let's go." Coach McNally guided the boys back to the street as they continued to ask questions about Boston University. Coach McNally mentioned to Corey it was like herding cattle to get the wandering boys back to the main street.

"How much does the school cost a year," asked Corey.

"Don't worry about that," said Travis. "We'll have scholarships."

"Travis, lets not get ahead of ourselves," added Coach McNally. "Corey, you work hard you will get far." Corey looked at Coach McNally. He smiled when coach nodded at him. "I was able to do it Corey, but that was 1987. Times have changed. You and Travis keep doing what your doing on the field, and I am sure the scouts will be watching you."

The boys looked at each other, and Corey regained confidence when Travis smiled at him.

"Scouts in two weeks baby," yelled Travis.

Corey smiled back at Travis. He returned his attention to Coach McNally. "How is BU looking this year anyway?"

Coach McNally pulled his phone from his pocket. Coach McNally led the boys into a discussion on Boston University players. Coach McNally went on to explain the season's schedule.

"Notre Dame is a good team, but I think BU will take it today," said Coach McNally. "BU has won their last three home games."

"I'm excited for today's game dad," said Travis. "I hope the running back makes a lot of good plays."

"You won't be disappointed," said Coach McNally. "Boston University has one of the best running backs in the state right now."

"How about the quarterback," asked Corey.

"He's good too," said Coach McNally. "He has had a few concussions since he's played for Boston though, so he tends to be more careful than he is confident."

Corey looked at Travis. Travis watched Corey sigh.

"Let's get going," said Travis. "The game is about to start."

Corey followed Travis and Coach McNally to the front of the bleachers. Notre Dame kicked off to Boston, and Travis screamed as the running back took it back to Boston University's forty-yard line. Corey and Travis fixed their eyes on the players, watching each play for precision and technique. When Corey questioned a move or play from either team, Coach McNally provided thorough answers with explicit details and examples. Corey continued to ask questions, and he noticed when Travis interrupted him. Corey wanted to ask Travis what his problem was, but Coach McNally ensured the Spartan quarterback that his questions were good questions. Coach McNally admitted that he wished Travis asked as many questions as Corey, and Corey watched Travis, and his friend said nothing.

Corey continued to ask questions as the game went into the second quarter. What formation did the offensive line usually play? Who were the top players for Boston? How many championships have they won? Travis yelled at his friend once to stop asking questions and watch the game, and Coach McNally

spoke firmly to Travis. Travis became quiet and Coach McNally

reminded Corey that his questions were appropriate questions.

Coach McNally advocated that Corey ask as many questions as he

wanted. Coach McNally reminded Travis that he should ask as

many questions and learn as much as possible. Corey watched

when Travis took steps to the left from him. He wanted to ask

Travis about it, but Corey did not want to ask him in public.

Corey watched as Travis kept to himself. The Spartan quarterback

refrained from asking further questions. Even though he was

curious and wanted to learn as he much as he could from the

game, Corey did not want any more drama with Travis. Corey

never liked when Travis was mad at him, and the quarterback

asked questions only when he thought they were smart enough

questions to interest even Travis. Corey looked at Travis each

time to see if his questions impressed his friend, and Travis

continued to look away.

As they watched the game like hawks, Corey and Travis

became well versed in Boston University's playbook by the

second half of the game. Before the third quarter, Coach McNally and the boys went to the concession stand to buy hot dogs and sodas. Coach McNally explained to them the complexity of the Boston v. Notre Dame rivalry, and though Corey was interested, Travis didn't add much to the conversation, and Coach McNally's conversations often fell off. Corey refrained from asking questions, and when Travis asked Coach McNally questions, Corey remained quiet to listen. Corey became envious of Travis, envious of Travis and his questions and his father and their love for each other and football. As Corey thought more about it, he kept to himself, nodding and affirming whatever Travis and Coach McNally were saying about Boston University.

The crowd began to cheer, and Travis led the way back to the bleachers. Corey, Travis, and Coach McNally watched as Boston kicked off to Notre Dame. When Notre Dame fumbled, Boston was able to take the ball back to the end zone. Corey, Travis, and Coach McNally screamed in joy over the play, and Corey became distracted from his sadness. Travis hit Corey on the shoulder, and Travis smiled at him. Corey smiled back at Travis, and the Spartan quarterback took two steps closer to his best friend.

By the fourth quarter, the boys were able to identify blitzes, in addition to running and passing plays. Boston and Notre Dame shut down each other's offensives quickly, and Notre Dame was only able to get a field goal during the quarter. With the final minutes on the clock, Boston University had the ball, and Corey noticed when the offense went into shotgun from an I formation. It was third and long. The coach and the two football players fell silent, and when the ball snapped, Boston's quarterback ran ten years behind the scrimmage line. Corey was sure the quarterback was going to get sacked, but the quarterback was able to escape the pocket, run to the edge of the sideline, and throw the ball to the tight end. The tight end landed in the end zone, and though he was tied up with a cornerback for the ball, the ball remained in his hands.

"Touchdown," screamed Coach McNally, rising from his seat.

Corey and Travis rose from their seats and shouted. Others around them followed.

"We just need to hold them back now and the game is ours," yelled Coach McNally.

Boston University was able to hold Norte Dame back, winning the game 28 - 24. As he promised, Coach McNally showed the boys around the school after the game. He pointed out his dorm room, two buildings where he took classes, and the practice football field.

"Why did you stop playing anyway coach," asked Corey.

"You and all the questions," said Travis.

"It's fine Travis," Coach McNally said. "To be honest Corey, I got injured. I tore my ACL."

"Sounds painful."

"It happens. College ball is the promise for some players, and the graveyard for others."

"Corey, you know my dad tore his ACL," said Travis. Travis looked at Corey. Travis then looked away.

"I'm sorry Travis, I just forgot," Corey said.

"I just wish you remembered more. You always ask the same questions."

Corey stared at Travis. Corey felt Coach McNally watching him. Corey became angry, but no sooner did he become sad and embarrassed.

"Leave him alone Travis, Corey is fine," Coach McNally finally said.

Corey held his feelings within, turning to his cell phone and social network for distractions. Travis pulled out his phone and did the same. Coach McNally observed the trees around him and took a deep breath. Coach McNally closed his eyes.

"Dad, how do we get back to the truck," asked Travis.

Coach McNally opened his eyes and pulled his phone from his pocket. "We'll need to take a train to South Station," said Coach McNally. "The truck is outside South Station."

Corey watched the trees race away as the train left Boston. When they reached the truck, Corey and Travis remained silent, and Coach McNally turned up the radio. Coach McNally heard a new song on the radio from the band he and Travis liked, and Corey was amused by Coach McNally's enthusiasm for the song. Coach McNally asked if Corey liked the song, and when Corey remained silent, Travis shared with his father that he liked the song.

Corey continued to wrestle what was going on with Travis. He decided that Travis wanted his father for himself.

Corey began to think that maybe he was taking his father away from Travis. Maybe it was not Corey's place to be so close and so needing of Coach McNally. Corey thought maybe he could ask Travis about it in private, and though it was not often he and Travis spoke in private, Corey decided sometime soon it would be good to clear his mind with his best and only friend.

"I hope you had a good time." Coach McNally shifted the truck into park and looked behind at Corey. Corey looked outside and realized he was at his house.

"I did, thank you for bringing me."

"See you Monday Corey," said Travis. Corey stared into Travis's eyes while he smiled. Corey smiled back.

No hard feelings, Corey thought, no hard feelings. "See you Monday Travis."

Corey waved as the truck drove off, and Corey watched the truck take a right off onto Grove Street. Corey entered the house, and when he realized his mother was not home, he called and left a message. The Spartan quarterback was in the shower when he heard the phone ring.

"Sorry Corey, I couldn't pick up. I'm at the house again."

"I thought you worked a double last night."

"I did, but they called me in this morning to help. There was an emergency."

Corey lifted his phone from his ear to look at the time. It was two in the afternoon.

"When are you coming home?"

"I will be home in the morning. There was an emergency and the house needs me to supervise tonight. How about we make pancakes in the morning?"

"I would like that."

"How was the game? I hope you had a good time."

"It was fun, Coach McNally and Travis were fun."

"Maybe I can go some time?"

Corey thought about the game Coach McNally was planning and Corey smiled. "Yes, I would like that."

"Sounds like a plan."

Corey thought about asking his mother about the emergency, but he fell silent on the phone.

"I have to go back to work Corey."

"Have you heard from dad," Corey asked quickly.

"We won't be hearing from dad for awhile."

"What he said about Coach McNally, I just don't believe it. He's such a nice guy."

"Don't believe it Corey. Don't let it bother you."

"But it bothers me."

Corey's mother sighed. Corey heard a male voice call Corey's mother over the phone.

"We will talk about it in the morning Corey, but I really need to go."

"Okay mom, I love you."

"I love you too Corey."

Corey hung up the phone. He watched recaps of the Boston and Notre Dame game in his room and studied college quarterbacks on his phone. The Spartan quarterback studied until the sun went down. Corey stumbled on an article discussing the cost of college, and he began to think of how he would pay $40,000 a year if he could not get a football scholarship. When he became anxious, Corey began to do push ups and sit-ups on his bedroom floor. When he became too sweaty, he took another shower. When he became too tired, Corey fell asleep.

Chapter Four

Corey awoke to the smell of fruit and chocolate coming out of the kitchen. When he found his mother starting pancakes, he guided her to the living room.

"I will take care of breakfast, you relax mom."

"Your such a good son Corey," his mother said. Corey's mother kissed him. Corey guided her to the couch and handed her the remote. Corey returned to the kitchen. Corey knew his mother liked cranberries and strawberries in her pancakes, and he made his own with chocolate chips.

"There's going to be scouts watching the game in two weeks mom," Corey said, handing her a plate.

"I bet you're excited."

Corey nodded.

"How is everything going with the Spartans? I hope everyone is treating you alright."

"It's going well, I think me and Travis are fitting right in."

Corey's mother scanned the television for something to watch. She stopped at her favorite station when she realized there was an episode to a soap opera she had not seen yet.

"I'm glad things are going well," Corey's mother said, looking at the television.

"You should come to the game in two weeks. I would really like it if you could make it."

"I will tell the house," Corey's mother said, still looking at the television. "I told Dr. Hamilton I'm looking for all the overtime I can get, but I will ask him about that Friday. What's the date?"

Corey looked on his phone. "November 13th. Please try mom. I would like you to see a game."

"I will try Corey."

Corey ate his pancakes with his mother. He cleaned the dishes after. He returned to watch television with her, and when she began nodding off to sleep, he turned the TV off and guided her to bed.

"Get some sleep mom. We can talk later."

Corey kissed his mother and closed the door of her bedroom. He dried off the dishes and went to shower. As he was drying off, Corey heard his phone ring, and he rushed to his phone before it could wake his mother.

"Hey Corey, " said Travis, "what are you up to?"

"Nothing much, just got out of the shower."

"Hey, I was wondering if you wanted to get together and practice. I'm feeling pumped from yesterday's game."

"I'm down."

"Okay cool, where do you wanna meet?"

"I don't know, where did you have in mind?"

"Can your mom bring you to the Spartan school?"

"Sorry man, she's sleeping. How about we meet at the Trojan's old practice field?"

Corey listened as Travis hesitated. Corey listened as Travis spoke with his father. He heard Coach McNally confirm he could drive Travis.

"I can be there in an hour," Travis said.

"Cool, see you then." Corey hung up the phone and changed back into gym shorts and his Boston University shirt from yesterday. He did not want to wake his mother so he left a note on her ashtray in the living room.

Out with Travis, be home at 5 to help with dinner, Love, Corey.

Coach McNally dropped Travis off at the old Trojan practice field. Corey asked why Coach McNally was leaving, and Travis insisted they train together. Corey realized it was not only him who wanted to speak in private. Corey thought about the rumor his father said about Travis's father. Corey wanted to tell Travis, but he did not want to upset his best friend. Instead, Corey let Travis speak his mind.

"Corey, I just wanted to say I'm sorry about yesterday."

"What do you mean?"

"About the questions you were asking my dad," Travis continued. "I guess I was getting jealous. I understand you don't really have a dad around right now."

Corey thought hard about Travis's words, but a part of him would not allow Travis to be sorry for him. Corey was ashamed of the anger he felt for Travis. He wanted to take Travis's words sincerely. Corey hated what he was feeling. The

Spartan quarterback hated Travis in this moment. Corey hated that Travis reminded him that he was disadvantaged. Corey could not allow Travis to be the fortunate one, even if he was the better athlete, even if he had the better father, even if he had the better probability of attending Boston University and becoming a professional football player. Corey didn't realize it, but he let out a loud shout. He knew he was worrying Travis when Travis put his hand on his shoulder. Corey swatted Travis's hand away and backed away from his best friend.

"Corey, I know you're mad, but we can talk this out."

Corey was too angry to listen. He took another step back from Travis. "Have you heard the rumors about your father Travis," Corey asked.

Travis looked at Corey with an agitated look. "What about my father?"

"Salvatore was telling me, but I didn't want to believe it."

"What about my father," Travis asked again, this time louder.

Corey stepped back and put his hands up, his palms facing Travis.

"Salvatore, my father, he was talking to Patrick's mother at the bar and I guess Patrick was telling her that Coach McNally was touching him, and that was the real reason your father left the Trojans. Do you think it's true?"

"What the fuck? Fuck no Corey," Travis yelled. "Where the fuck did you hear this shit?"

"Salvatore, my father," Corey said. "Patrick's mother was telling him at the bar."

"The bar," Travis asked with a dark laugh. "Well, Patrick's mother is a dumb bitch."

"Yeah, I didn't believe it either," Corey said. Corey watched Travis pace back and forth. Corey felt guilt and satisfaction as Travis paced. Corey felt Travis was now down to his level, a disadvantaged boy alongside him.

Travis continued to pace. Travis then faced Corey. "Let's all talk tonight," Travis finally said. "For now, how about we run some suicides?"

Corey was irritated Travis was ready to dismiss the conversation so quickly, but Corey did not have anything to add to the discussion. Corey agreed to run Travis's suicides. Corey even tried to race Travis, but Travis would not race him back. Corey thought his anger would last after suicides, but the activity exhausted Corey, and Corey lost his aggression. Travis suggested they sit at the bleachers and Corey was more than happy to.

Travis called his father. "Hey dad, how about we grab a pizza with Corey? There are some things I think we should talk about."

Travis hung up his phone and looked at Corey.

"I told my mother I would be home at five to help with dinner," Corey said.

"Have her come along with us," Travis said. "Maybe she can help us get to the bottom of this."

Corey pulled out his phone and called his mother. She was waking up. Corey's mother told Corey she would meet them. When Corey said Coach McNally was going to be there, his mother asked him what she should wear, and Corey snapped at his mother. Corey told her this was not a date. Travis looked over at Corey. When Travis laughed at Corey, Corey laughed at himself.

"Meet us at Leo's for seven," Corey said. Corey's mother agreed and he hung up his phone. Corey and Travis spent ten minutes looking at their phones, maintaining their distractions. When Travis suggested they pass a football around, Corey put his phone away, following Travis back to the field. Corey and Travis threw a football around until Coach McNally's truck pulled into the parking lot.

Chapter Five

The pizza shop was empty when Coach McNally and the boys

settled in. Corey's mother arrived as the pizza was coming out.

When Coach McNally introduced himself, he called Corey's

mother Eileen and she reminded him it was Emily, and they

laughed. Corey noticed his mother's red sweatshirt was tight

around her chest, and Corey felt uncomfortable.

"I'm guessing this is about Sal," Emily asked.

"Yeah," Coach McNally said. "Where is he anyway?"

"He's out of town, staying with a friend."

"Coward," Travis added.

"These rumors Emily, I hope you know they're not true."

"I never did believe them Jeff. Helen has been running her

mouth at the bar."

"Bitch," Travis snorted.

"What does she have against you anyway coach," asked

Corey.

Coach McNally passed around the plates and everyone

took a slice of pizza.

"It's Patrick's father, Coach Galanos," Coach McNally said. "He's been trying to get one of his friends to be his offensive coach ever since Corey's grandfather passed. See, when Corey's grandfather retired, he wanted me to head coach the Trojans. Well, the principal wouldn't have that, and naturally things became worse when the old man passed."

"But to say you touch boys," exclaimed Travis. "What kind of shit is that?"

"I honestly don't think Coach Galanos would say that," Coach McNally said. "I honestly think that rumor is coming from Helen. With everything that went down at Penn State a few years ago, I guess it was rumor she thought people would believe."

"I think you're right," Corey's mother said. "When Sal and I were at the bar talking to her, Galanos was not even with her."

"He was not there," said Coach McNally, his voice raised in pitch. "When did you see Helen at the bar anyway?"

"I don't know, some time in early August."

"Have you seen her since then?"

"Yeah, but I really don't want to talk about it."

Corey looked at his mother and a rage engulfed him. Corey held his anger within.

"Sorry ma," said Travis, "but this is not a time to really not want to talk about it." Corey watched Travis as he glared at his mother with madness in his eyes. "We are talking about my father's reputation here."

Corey's mother looked at Corey. As she looked away, she shook her head. "I saw Helen a few weeks ago. It was after Sal and I had a fight over Corey transferring schools."

"Okay, and where did you see her," Travis asked.

"I saw her at the Cove. See, what happened was Sal and I got into a fight and-"

"And what," screamed Travis.

Coach McNally insisted Travis be respectful. Travis settled back into his seat.

Corey's mother was looking at Corey again. "Anyway, when Sal and I got into a fight, I was going to the Cove to get a drink. Sal and I usually went to the other side of town to get a drink, and I thought I would be able to get a drink at the Cove without anyone seeing me. Well, it turned out that Sal and Helen were meeting at the Cove."

"Did you see them," Coach McNally asked.

"What did you say," added Travis.

Corey's mother looked at Corey again. "I did see them but I didn't talk to them. I saw them through the window and I turned around and went home." Corey's mother looked at Corey again. "I'm sorry Corey."

Corey's mother excused herself and went outside for a cigarette. Corey rose from his seat to go with her, but his mother gestured for him to stay. "I will be right back," Corey's mother said. "I just need a minute."

Corey returned to his seat.

"Now I don't know what to believe," Travis said.

"I'm guessing you didn't know about all this Corey," said Coach McNally.

Corey didn't reply to Coach McNally. The Spartan quarterback had a sudden urge to run away. He thought about leaving, but there was nowhere to go. He would have to work through this, he thought. Corey listened to Coach McNally and

Travis talk about the rumor, and the quarterback listened until he could hear no more of it.

"I don't think we should worry too much about this rumor stuff," Corey said. "We are Spartans now. What can Coach Galanos or Helen do to us now?"

"I think you're right," Coach McNally said.

"But these rumors," added Travis. "Dad, you don't want these rumors spreading into the Spartan team."

"Yeah, you're right Travis." Corey watched as Coach McNally went into deep though. Corey watched as Coach McNally rose from his seat. "Boys, I'm going to talk to Emily, you wait here." Corey and Travis watched as Coach McNally walked away. Corey questioned Coach McNally's motive.

"I'm sorry Corey, it's not fair your mother didn't tell you," was the only thing Travis could say.

Corey was at a loss for words. Corey watched Coach McNally and his mother return to the table, and he noticed something changed. Coach McNally and his mother were now sitting together. Corey watched as Coach McNally offered her another slice of pizza. Corey watched as his mother declined.

"How about you boys take the pizza and go on to the house," Coach McNally said. "I think me and Emily need some more time to talk alone."

Coach McNally threw his keys to Travis. "I know you don't know where you're going," Coach McNally said. "Let me see your phone." Coach McNally took Travis's phone and put their address into his GPS.

"Take the car and we will talk tomorrow."

"How are you going to get home," asked Travis.

"I will bring him back," Emily said.

Corey and Travis felt the same emotion - hesitation. Travis walked out of the pizza shop without saying goodbye to his father or Emily. Corey looked at Coach McNally and then at his mother. He would have hugged and kissed his mother and told her that he loved her, but he was too upset to say anything to Emily.

The boys returned to Travis's house and they tried to talk. When it became too uncomfortable, they distracted themselves with their phones. Travis asked Corey if he wanted to continue with their characters on his new football game, and Corey agreed.

The boys finished their season undefeated. After winning two

games in the post season, they shut the game off. Travis went into

his room to sleep and Corey rested on the living room couch.

Corey attempted to sleep, but when he had a terrible nightmare

about his father, he awoke in sweat. Corey tried to splash water

on himself in the bathroom and pace around the living room, but

Corey's anxiety continued. Corey wanted to wake up Travis, and

at one point Corey thought he would have to go to the hospital,

but Corey did not want to disrupt his best friend. Corey lied

awake on the living room floor and shivered until sleep finally

possessed him.

Chapter Six

Corey watched the next two weeks past, waking and sleeping like he had for sixteen years. When November 13th came around, Corey woke up any other Friday morning. Corey showered, brushed his teeth, and listened to his music. When he put on his jersey for school that Friday morning, he felt a sense of pride and passion, and this was something new. Corey felt a pride and passion knowing that in a few hours he would be playing for Boston University scouts, moving one step closer to his dream.

Emily drove Corey into school like every other morning. She opened up to Corey about the things she was telling Coach McNally at Leo's Pizza, and though he loved her, Corey did not completely trust his mother anymore. Corey began to wonder if she was really working all those overtime hours at the Trojan Residential House. Corey began to wonder if it was really Dr. Hamilton in the background when she was talking to him on the phone. Either way, Corey was happy when Coach McNally asked his mother to get dinner and drinks, and at least during those times Corey knew where his mother was. At least during those times, Corey knew what his mother was doing, and that she was safe. He was also happy that his mother was going to see him play for the scouts tonight. He was happy that she was going to go to the Boston University game with him, Travis, and Coach McNally tomorrow morning.

Though Corey had things to be happy about that Friday, the sky was full of clouds when he arrived at school, and he spent most of his classes watching the dark dreary clouds through classroom windows. As each class went by, he focused less and less on what his teachers were saying. Even after lunch, the clouds did not cease and the sun did not show itself. The clouds began to make Corey think of his father. Corey remembered those times that his father beat him, and Corey remembered vividly that first summer evening when his father began beating him with plates. Corey remembered that his father had really beaten him with plates. Corey remembered this was five years ago. Corey remembered it was not just a nightmare he had one night sleeping over Travis's house.

Corey met Travis after school in the locker room, and as Travis spoke to Corey, his mind began to clear. The boys spoke about what they would do if a scout found them tonight, and they began to imagine themselves living in the same dorm building overlooking the stadium, just like Coach McNally during his Boston University years. The boys began to imagine living in the same dorm room and living the same life Coach McNally lived during his college years. Corey and Travis envisioned themselves practicing on the same practice field. Corey and Travis envisioned themselves impressing the older football players like they did when they were Trojans, and later when they became Spartans. The boys even envisioned themselves winning the Super Bowl and both of them earning Rookie of the Year. Coach McNally grounded the boys back to reality when the Spartan team began to review St. John's playbook, and when Travis began taking mental notes, Corey followed.

Corey and Travis followed the Spartan seniors into the gym for calisthenics, and as Corey began to move, his heart and mind became as one. The sweat on his face gave him joy, and when he looked at Travis by his side, he forgot his earlier worries, focusing again on his dream with Travis. Tonight, Corey thought, scouts would be watching him and Travis. Tonight would be the first night of their future, their dream realized. Corey focused on his vaulting ambitions with Travis, and when they practiced plays, Corey and Travis exploded from the line. After warm ups, Coach McNally announced the boys would start the first quarter. Corey thought the seniors would become upset, but when the entire team met for one last time before the game, the seniors honored Corey and Travis's commitment to the game, and the boys exploded in passion.

"Let's do this baby," said Travis, crashing his facemask into Corey's.

Corey slammed his facemask back into Travis's, "Let's do this!"

Corey and Travis followed the Spartan seniors as the team ran out onto the football field. The crowd screamed to them as they ran. Corey looked into the bleachers to find his mother. When he did not see her, he thought maybe it was still early. Maybe she was still on her way. Travis put his arm around Corey and whispered to him.

"Those three men up there in burgundy sweatshirts," Travis said. "Those are the BU scouts baby." Travis waved to them and Corey grabbed his arm to stop him.

"Don't be that guy," Corey said. "Let them see what you got on the field."

Travis nodded his head and sprinted forward. Corey followed. Corey looked into the bleachers one more time then turned away. Corey focused now on only what was right in front of him.

During the first quarter, the Spartan defense dominated St. John's offense. When the Spartan offense took the field, they struggled to make gains. Corey had a handful of successful passes, and Travis made a few successful runs, but St. John's defense was as strong as it was big. The Spartans were unable to score any touchdowns the first quarter, but they were able to position their kicker to earn a field goal. When the first quarter ended, the Spartans were at 3 and St. John's was at 7.

When the second quarter began, the Spartan defense was on the field. Corey looked again through the bleachers to find his mother, but he could not. When Travis saw Corey looking around, he insisted that she was there, and that they just could not see her.

"I'm sure she's up there somewhere Corey," Travis said. "Just keep your focus. Please keep your focus. Look, the scouts are watching."

St. John's offense was able to make two first downs, but they were unable to score before the Spartan offense returned to the field. Coach McNally called Corey to run a series of slant and screen passes, and when they were successful, Travis found momentum on the field, running a series of draw and off tackle rushes. Before the quarter was out, Travis was able to rush in two touchdowns. During the last touchdown, Corey made an important block that was the key factor to Travis getting into the end zone. Corey didn't admit it to Coach McNally or Travis, but when he made the block, he was hit hard, and Corey became dizzy.

The team regrouped in the outside locker room at half time, and Corey watched as his teammates praised him. Corey felt exhilarated by the praise, and Corey and Travis exchanged a hug. Coach McNally quieted the team, and though the Spartans were up 17 to 7, the coach reminded the players that the game was still young and anybody could take it. Corey and Travis looked at each other and confirmed Coach McNally's words. Coach McNally

continued that to start the third quarter, Corey would sit out.

Coach McNally made a reference to Corey's block, and Corey

had the opportunity to admit he was still dizzy, but Corey did not

want to disappoint the team. Corey accepted the applause by his

teammates. Travis whispered to Corey that it was probably a good

idea that Corey took a quarter off, saving his arm for the last

quarter so he could really impress the scouts. Corey smiled along

with Travis, confirming with Travis, whatever Travis was saying.

Corey shook hands with the senior starting quarterback and

wished him luck. Corey, Travis, and the senior starting

quarterback led the way back to the field. The crowd screamed for

the Spartans.

Corey spent much of the third quarter on the bench. When

he began to feel dizzier, he rose to get water. While he was

getting water, Corey noticed a man in the bleachers wearing a

green and gold varsity jacket. He did not see the man's face

because he was turned around, but Corey recognized the jacket

and the year, 1965. Corey turned away quickly before the man

could turn around, and after Corey drank his cup of water, he forced his helmet back on. Corey began to feel sweat on his face. Corey began to feel his hands shake. Corey rose from the bench and paced back and forth until Travis returned to the sideline.

"What's wrong Corey," Travis asked.

"I think I saw my father."

"Your father? How do you know it was him?"

"He was wearing my grandfather's varsity jacket, 1965 super bowl champions."

"Did you see his face or did you just see his jacket?"

"I just saw his jacket."

Travis sighed and then smiled toward Corey, placing his arm on his shoulder. "I bet it was someone else Corey," Travis said. "Your grandfather was not the only one to get a varsity jacket in 65' you know."

"Maybe you're right," said Corey, "yeah Travis, I think you're right."

Corey watched as Travis talked to Coach McNally with the start of the fourth quarter. Corey tried to watch the Spartan defense, but he could not focus, his mind half dizzy, his mind half obsessed about the green and gold varsity jacket. Corey wished he could look behind him and see his mother, but he was convinced now that she was not there, and that she was called in at the house for another emergency, or something. Corey recalled and remembered his first emergency five years ago, and Corey felt his body shake vigorously for half a minute.

Corey didn't notice, but the Spartan defense returned to the sidelines. Travis ran to Corey, and when Corey wasn't listening to what he was saying, Travis pulled him from his arm and raised Corey up to his feet. "Let's go Corey! Your back in the game!"

Corey ran out to the field with Travis and the rest of the offense. Coach McNally signaled Corey to run an off tackle rush, and Travis exploded from the line, earning the Spartan offense fifteen yards. Coach McNally then called Corey to run a screen, and Travis was able to get the offense another ten yards. As the Spartan offense was within twenty feet of the end zone, Corey took the snap from the center like he did for any other draw. When he handed the ball to Travis, Corey fumbled, following the ball ten yards behind the line of scrimmage. Corey heard yelling all around him, and in panic, Corey gripped the ball and attempted to run. Corey ran five yards before a linebacker stopped

him. When he was hit, Corey flipped backwards, falling on his

head. Travis ran to Corey and tried to help him up, but Corey did

not respond. Coach McNally screamed for the EMTs, and

medical professionals ran onto the field. When Corey continued

to not respond, an ambulance took him away. The Spartan

quarterback was sent to the hospital.

Chapter Seven

Travis and Coach McNally visited Corey the night after the game. Corey was still unconscious in the hospital, and Corey's mother insisted the two of them go the Boston University game Saturday and visit Corey on Sunday. When Corey awoke Saturday night, his mother was by his side, and Corey cried endlessly to her.

Corey's mother cradled Corey's head and helped him return to the world. Corey continued to cry until he could speak. Corey's mother tried to tell him she was at the game. Emily tried to tell Corey she was watching him, but Corey could not understand. When he could speak, Corey told his mother he was sorry his father got so upset about him not wanting to play football anymore when he was ten. Corey told his mother that he was sorry his father hit him with grandma's plates when he was too angry with him. Corey's mother wanted to cry along with her son, but she did not want to see him get worse. Corey's mother knew Corey could be worse. Corey's mother had seen Corey, and she knew his worst. When it was too much to bear, the lawyer and the doctor pulled Emily away from Corey. The doctor called a nurse to tend Corey, and the doctor guided Corey's mother and the lawyer to a side room where there was a desk and chairs to discuss Corey's future.

"I'm sorry Emily," the doctor said, "but your son is finished. The amount of trauma he has, and now a severe concussion. Corey won't be able to return to the world and function like you and me."

"Corey has done it before," Corey's mother cried, "and I am confident he can do it again."

"I'm sorry Emily," said the lawyer, "but the Department can no longer allow you or Salvatore to have custody of Corey. We've been watching Sal since he beat up Corey five years ago, and I think we were pretty clear on our expectations. We had told you last time that with Corey's trauma, he should not be playing football anymore."

"But I have done nothing wrong," cried Corey's mother. "You can't take Corey away from me!"

"It doesn't matter Emily," said the lawyer. "The Department can no longer trust you or Salvatore as safe guardians for Corey. We gave you the chance five years ago, but we can't trust that you will do the right thing for Corey. We will find a placement for Corey, and when we do, you will be able to visit him. When he turns eighteen and if he wants to sign out and live with you, that is his decision."

"But all Corey ever wanted was to play football."

"That's what Salvatore wanted," said the lawyer. "Now I know it doesn't sound right Emily, but it doesn't matter anymore what Corey wants with his life. Right now, the Department is concerned on what Corey needs."

Emily looked at the lawyer and then at the doctor. Corey's mother ran out of the room. The lawyer looked at the doctor. Neither of the men moved from their seats.

The lawyer looked up to the ceiling then over to the doctor. "Everyday in America there is a youth swallowed up by tragedy," said the lawyer, "but let me ask you doc. How many people you think will ever read about the fall of Corey?"

Made in the USA
Charleston, SC
12 May 2016